★ ★ HOT
OF THE
GODS

For Ross, who is as clever as Loki,
but much, much nicer.

ORCHARD BOOKS

First published in Great Britain in 2023 by Hodder & Stoughton

1 3 5 7 9 10 8 6 4 2

Text © Hodder & Stoughton Limited 2023
Cover and inside illustrations by Stephen Brown and Advocate Art Ltd
© Hodder & Stoughton Limited 2023
Extra illustrations © Shutterstock

A CIP catalogue record for this book is available from the British Library.

ISBN 978 1 40836 556 4

Printed in Great Britain

The paper and board used in this book are made from
wood from responsible sources

Orchard Books
An imprint of Hachette Children's Group
Part of Hodder & Stoughton Limited
Carmelite House, 50 Victoria Embankment, London EC4Y 0DZ

An Hachette UK Company
www.hachette.co.uk
www.hachettechildrens.co.uk

HOTEL
OF THE
GODS

VIKINGS ON VACATION

BY TOM EASTON

ORCHARD

CHAPTER ONE

*T*his is **FABULOUS**, Atlas thought to himself as he lay back on his sun lounger, looking out across the lush grounds of the Hotel of the Gods. *I actually live here. In this grand hotel, amongst the most beautiful gardens you could ever imagine, full of animals, flowers and magic.*

A little dog came trotting up and plopped a slobbery tennis ball between the two sun loungers occupied by Atlas and his companion.

This is **AMAZING,** Atlas thought to himself as he threw the ball across the neat, clipped lawn. Cerbie the dog raced after it, yapping like a maniac, then came back with the ball and dropped it once more, grinning up at Atlas. *I finally have my own pet.*

Cerbie's real name was Cerberus, and until fairly recently he'd lived in the hotel basement with Hades, the Greek god of the

dead. You'd never guess
that he was really a three-
headed hellhound.

Atlas's companion reached down for the
ball and flexed his tattooed, muscled arm
ready to throw it. *This is* **INCREDIBLE**,
Atlas thought. *Just me hanging out with my
best friend Māui, who is probably the coolest
and most fun person I've ever met, and who also
just happens to be a demigod.* Māui launched
the ball high into the air with a sound like a
cracking whip.

"Whoa," Māui said with a chuckle. "That
ball is really moving, dude."

Atlas frowned. Māui was right. It *was*

moving, still heading up. In fact, the ball was rocketing at such a speed that it caught fire and left a trail of black smoke across the sky. Eventually the trail curled downwards and the ball dropped at supersonic speed over the swimming pool, across the lawns and towards the stables.

Atlas winced and clenched his shoulders as he anticipated what was to come next. Sure enough, the ball punched through the roof of the stables and exploded with a loud **BANG**, great plumes of flame punching out the windows and door. Pegasus appeared at the door and stared at them accusingly, his wings singed.

"**Sorry, bro!**" Māui shouted.

Atlas shook his head. It was fun having the Polynesian hero as his best friend, but sometimes Māui's trickster nature could be a bit difficult, to be honest. There was quite a lot of smothering fires with blankets, fulsome apologies and a fair few singed eyebrows – and wings – along the way.

Atlas had been living at the Hotel of the Gods for a few months now. He and his sister Ari (short for Ariadne), had escaped their humdrum lives in grey and grimy Midham when their mum and dad got themselves jobs as manager and chef here. Their new lives had seemed too good to be true.

And truthfully, things hadn't always run completely smoothly, especially when Atlas had accidentally opened the gates of hell and three horrifying creatures escaped from mythology and firmly into reality. It was only through a lot of luck and a few bruises that Atlas had managed to get them back under lock and key. Well, apart from Cerbie, who'd ended up becoming his pet.

"Should we go and check the stables?" Atlas asked.

"Nah, it's too hot to get up," Māui said, stretching out on the lounger, his long black locs spread out around his head.

"What if the building burns to the

ground?" Atlas asked, biting his thumbnail.

"Then we'll rebuild it," Māui said, shrugging. "Further away this time. Pegasus poo stinks."

The chattering of Ari and Venus distracted Atlas. He looked over to see them approaching the pool in swimwear. Venus's long red hair was coiled around her head in a braid.

"Not like them to go for a swim," Māui said. "Especially considering what's in the pool."

"They're not here for a swim," Atlas replied. He knew Ari, and he'd come to know Venus too. The girls were very similar in lots of ways: one of them was a **FIERCE** and **POWERFUL** woman and the other was a **FIERCE** and **POWERFUL** Roman goddess. Venus, the goddess of love and beauty, ran the hotel salon and had adopted Ari as her apprentice. But in fact they spent most of the time doing their nails and chatting. Ari loved to hear stories about what the gods got up to in ancient times. They didn't have many customers, because most of the residents of the hotel took care of their own grooming. Bastet, the Egyptian cat goddess, spent most of her waking hours cleaning herself, like any good cat. Thor and Mars spent hours in front of the mirror every morning, first doing their hair, then lifting weights in the gym, bickering over which of them was the strongest, most powerful and most handsome.

The salon did occasionally get a visit from Hades when he came up from the basement to get his hair dyed jet black. But only when he was expecting a visit from his wife, Persephone.

No, Ari and Venus had a lot of free time. And today they seemed to want to spend it sunbathing.

"Atlas!" Ari shouted crossly from across the pool.

"What?" Atlas called back.

"Can you clean up your dog's mess, please? I nearly stepped in it," his sister said.

Atlas rolled his eyes and pulled a poo bag out of his pocket. He walked around the swimming pool to where the girls had positioned themselves.

"It's everywhere!" Ari complained as he took care of the job.

"Well, it's not just three heads he has . . ." Atlas pointed out.

Ari glared at him. He stuck out his tongue and pulled another ball from his pocket.

"Come on, Cerbie!" he called.

The girls settled down to sunbathe. Māui and Atlas began throwing the new ball back and forth while Cerbie bounded around yelping and slobbering like mad.

"Do you have to do that here?" Ari snapped, wiping a drop of dog drool off her arm. "It's a big garden."

"Do you have to sunbathe here?" Atlas responded. "It's a big sun."

"At least go back over to the other side of the pool," Ari said coldly. "We want to talk without **ANNOYING LITTLE BOYS** overhearing."

Atlas was about to protest and was surprised when Māui pulled him away. It wasn't like Māui to walk away from an opportunity to cause trouble. But once over the other side of the pool, Māui winked at Atlas and pulled a hook-shaped object out of his colourful board shorts. It looked like it was made from bone or smooth coral.

"This is my magic fish-hook," Māui whispered.

"How is it magic?" Atlas asked.

"I'll show you." Māui attached a length of fishing line to the hook, spun it around his head a few times then tossed it high into the air, towards one of the scattered clouds. Atlas blinked in surprise to see the hook catch

hold of the cloud. Māui began hauling the
fishing line, dragging the cloud across the sky
and lower down until it ended up right over
the girls' sun loungers.

Venus sat up, looking at the cloud crossly,
then she saw the fishing line and whipped
her head around to glare at Māui.

"Māui!" she snapped. Then, with a wave
of her hand, she broke the line and the cloud
floated away. Māui giggled.

17

"Sunbathing," he huffed. "What a waste of time." He lay back down on the lounger and sighed happily.

"But we're sunbathing too," Atlas said.

"Wrong, little dude," Māui replied. "We're waiting."

"What for?"

"The right moment to play our next trick." Māui held out a fist and opened it, showing Atlas what he had inside.

"A spider?" Atlas asked. "Ari and Venus aren't going to be scared of a little spider."

"Maybe not a *little* spider," Māui said with a sly grin.

He stood and, ducking down, circled

around the pool, hiding from view, though Atlas could see the girls were completely ignoring them in any case as they lay flat out, sunglasses on, soaking up some rays. Atlas followed Māui. Part of him felt a bit bad playing tricks like this. But it was only a small part. Māui's tricks were hilarious, and Ari deserved it, especially after the "little boys" comment.

Māui hunkered down and dropped the tiny spider on to the grass, where it stopped for a moment, feelers twitching. Atlas watched Māui wave a hand over the small arachnid then step back hurriedly as it began to grow.

FAST!

"Whoa!" Atlas said, backing away.
The spider grew, and grew, and grew,
until it was twice the height of Atlas.
Its huge hairy legs drummed on the ground,
then Māui slapped it on the bottom and it
shot off towards the pool, in the direction of
the girls.

"Oh, Venus!" Māui called. "Your
boyfriend's here!"

Venus sat up and turned her head.
"*AAAAAAGGGH!*" she shrieked. Ari's
head popped up too and she joined in the
shrieking, in perfect harmony. Then the
girls were up and scrambling, upturning sun
loungers in their wake. Into the pool they

went. *SPLASH!*

The two girls popped up, spluttering and splashing in the murky water, covered in green algae.

"My hair!" Ari shouted.

"*My nails*!" Venus screamed. She saw Māui falling about laughing. "*YOU*!" she shouted.

The spider shrank as the spell wore off. But then Atlas saw something rising out of the water behind the girls. He knew just what it was: the great scaly head of a water dragon. The dragon's name was Sìǎhai Lóngwáng, the Dragon King, but Atlas secretly called him Old Grumpy. He was the reason no one ever swam in the pool. Atlas had had a narrow

run-in with him before, and there wasn't anything that could entice him to get back into that pool, thinking about those teeth and that enormous tail.

"Ari," he cried out. "Behind you!"

"I'm not falling for that," Ari snapped crossly.

"No, really," Atlas said, pointing at the great water beast who was heading towards the girls menacingly, a plume of water rising in his wake.

"I expect tricks from Māui," Ari said, "but my own brother?"

"IT'S NOT A TRICK!" Atlas yelled.

"Uh oh," Māui muttered.

But then it was too late. Atlas's eyes widened as the dragon's tail rose high out of the pool before crashing down. A huge wave lifted the girls out of the water and cast them sprawling on to the poolside, where they lay coughing.

"*Māui*!" Venus screamed in fury.

"*ATLAS*!" Ari shouted, incensed.

"**Let's go!**" Māui spluttered.

The boys went running across the lawn in fits of giggles. *This is* **BRILLIANT!** thought Atlas. Life was never dull around Māui.

CHAPTER TWO

As they neared the main hotel building, they heard the sound of the dinner bell.

"**FOOD!**" Māui cried, delighted, as they headed towards the dining room. "Your dad is the **BEST** cook."

Atlas nodded. Everyone loved his dad's food.

As they went into the dining room, they saw a sign which read:

AZTEC NITE TONITE!

"Oh man, this day just keeps getting better," Māui said. "I love Mexican food, especially that awesome corn on the cob thing your dad does."

A voice came from behind them, making Atlas jump. "Did I ever tell you it was me who taught the Aztec people to grow corn?"

"Yes, Quetzalcóatl." Māui sighed as they joined the queue for the plates. "Only about a thousand times." Atlas always felt uneasy around Quetzalcóatl, the large Aztec god whose true form was a huge feathered serpent – though right now he was in roughly human form, albeit with a long, feathered headdress.

"Though they called it maize," Quetzalcóatl went on.

"WhatEVER," Māui said, his eyes rolling.

"We know," Atlas said politely. Quetzalcóatl could be so boring.

"Corn goes terribly well with roasted human flesh," the Aztec god added.

Atlas's eyes widened.

You had to be on your guard around Quetzalcóatl. The ancient Aztecs used to make human sacrifices to him, and Atlas sometimes saw the god eyeing him up hungrily . . .

Hades arrived. Atlas had got to know the god of the underworld quite well in his first week at the hotel. But after a tricky start they'd become good friends, and in fact Atlas's dog Cerbie was really Hades's three-headed hellhound Cerberus, who sometimes guarded the gates of hell when he wasn't lying on the rug in front of the **FIRE OF RELENTLESS TORMENT** having his belly scratched.

Hades was trying to reinvent himself as a fun person in order to fit in more with the other hotel residents. He called the surface world "Upstairs" and lately had been spending more and more time up here instead of in the basement. He told terrible jokes, played the guitar in a band of demons

and recently had taken to producing wall
hangings with inspirational sayings on them.
His latest work was on display in the lobby.
It read:

In This Hotel
We Make Mistakes.
We Say Sorry.
We Take Immortal Souls.
We Give Hugs.
We Doom People to Eternal
Damnation.
We Forgive.
We Kidnap Persephone and Drag
Her Down to the Underworld.
We LOVE.

Māui and Atlas managed to escape from Quetzalcóatl and found a table with a bored-looking Thor, who was eating a taco whilst idly tossing his hammer and catching it by the handle. They put their heaped plates down in front of them, full of beans and pork and tortillas and rice and sour cream.

Hades came to join them. Māui glanced at him with a frown. Some of the gods hadn't completely warmed to Hades yet.

"I see we're joined by the god of death," Māui said.

"Actually," Hades said sniffily, "I am not the god of death, I am the god of the dead."

"What's the difference?" Māui asked.

"It's my role to represent the interests of the dead. I'm like a spokesperson for them. They're very misunderstood."

Before they could begin eating, the doors to the garden burst open with a bang and someone flew in, landing with a thud and skidding to a stop on the polished floor. Everyone looked up to see a curly-haired figure in a hi-vis bib standing there.

It was Hermes, the slightly unreliable messenger of the gods. He unrolled a scroll and cleared his throat, only to be interrupted by a cry from Mars across the room.

"Oi, Hermes. Where's my parcel got to? I've been waiting for my new spear sharpener for over two weeks."

"It's coming, it's coming," Hermes snapped. "Supply chain issues!" He glared at Mars.

"Hermes would make a terrible stand-up comedian," Hades said.

Atlas raised an eyebrow. "Why's that?"

"Because," said Hades, "comedy is all in the delivery. And he's never on time!"

As Hades leaned back in his chair, laughing at his own joke, Hermes began speaking:

"Here follows a message from Odin, the one-eyed king of the Norse gods of Asgard, to his son, Thor: I grow tired of the trickster Loki and have suggested he spend some time away at the Hotel of the Gods. He will join you for your Midsummer's Night Celebration."

A great murmuring went up from the dinner guests.

Thor dropped his hammer with a clank. "Oh no," he muttered.

Hermes went on, "I thought it only fair to warn you. Since he's such a pain in the backside. Message ends."

Māui clapped Thor on the back, a great

grin on his face. "Loki is coming!" he said. "That should liven things up a bit!"

"You can say that again," Thor said, a worried look on his handsome face.

★ CHAPTER ★
THREE

"This is very exciting," Mum said, rushing over to the table where Atlas and Māui were scoffing their food. Thor sat quietly, toying with his taco and looking thoughtful.

"A new guest, and just in time for the **MIDSUMMER'S NIGHT CELEBRATION**," added Ari, coming over to join in.

"**Just in time to party!**" Māui said,

grinning and nodding his head.

Thor just grunted.

"You don't seem very excited," Ari said. "Isn't Loki your brother?"

"He is NOT my brother," Thor huffed. "Everyone thinks that, but we aren't related. I can't think of two people less alike! We've never gotten along."

"Siblings don't always get along," Ari said, glaring at Atlas. It seemed she still hadn't forgiven him for the spider incident.

"We haven't had a new guest for some time," Māui said thoughtfully.

"How long has it been?" Atlas asked.

Māui thought for a while. "Hard to

remember exactly, but maybe a thousand years?"

"A thousand years?!" Atlas exclaimed.

"Give or take a century or two," Māui said, shrugging. "History isn't my strong suit."

"We must get on with the preparations," Mum went on. "We'll have bunting, and games, and dancing. Perhaps Hades can bring his band of demons to play again?" Hades had a mouth full of food, but gave a thumbs up.

"What does Loki like to eat?" Dad asked, arriving at the table. "I shall make him his favourite dish."

"What does he look like?" Ari asked.

"It will be nice to have a new face around here," Venus added. "One grows terribly tired of the same old faces with their same old boring stories." She glanced over to Mars as she said this. Her boyfriend, the Roman god of war, was sitting on the other side of the room, trying to balance a crossbow on his nose.

But Thor had still not spoken. "What's wrong, Thor?" Atlas asked. "Aren't you looking forward to seeing Loki?"

Thor sighed. "We grew up together," he said. "There is a reason Odin sent him away. He is a **trickster**. A **joker**. A **player of games**."

"He sounds like a **total legend**," Māui said.

"He is NOT a legend," Thor said, banging

his huge fist on the table. "**He is . . . a big meanie**."

Everyone looked at each other, shocked. They weren't used to Thor being anything other than positive and cheerful.

"What do you mean?" Ari asked gently.

"He's very clever," Thor said. "And he likes to make me feel stupid."

"But you ARE stupid, bro," Māui said, patting Thor's shoulder.

"He always gets me into trouble with

Odin," Thor went on. "There was this one time when he painted Yggdrasil, the World Tree, with glow-in-the-dark paint. Odin was furious when he found out. He brought us all into the great hall and turned off the lights. Well, Loki had only gone and splashed some of the paint on my shoe and everyone saw it glowing in the dark. They all blamed me and Odin buried me under a mountain for a hundred years."

"That's terrible," Ari said.

"Then there was the time he told the **ICE GIANTS** that I was responsible for climate change because I kept lighting my farts with a flaming torch, and they kidnapped me and buried me under an ice mountain for a hundred years."

"That's awful," Atlas said.

"But the worst time of all was when he stole my hammer and replaced it with one of those rubber ones that squeaks when you hit something."

"That's . . . hilarious," Māui said.

"It wasn't hilarious when we went into battle against the **DARK ELVES** and I bonked the elf general on the head with it," Thor growled.

"Actually, that does sound pretty funny," Hades said.

"Odin was furious," Thor continued. "He

buried me under a mountain of dung for a hundred years."

"You do seem to get buried under mountains a lot," Mum said, patting Thor on his beefy shoulder.

"Loki is the reason I spend most of my time here, at the Hotel of the Gods," Thor said. "Apart from the great food, of course." He gave Atlas's dad a quick fist-bump, which nearly knocked Dad off his feet.

"We're glad to have you here," said Mum.

"Yeah, but now he's coming here. And I don't know if anyone else has noticed this, but . . ." Thor waved vaguely towards the dining room windows. "There are a LOT of mountains around the hotel."

"Maybe he's mellowed in the years since you've seen him," Atlas suggested.

"I doubt it," Thor said grimly. "Every time you think Loki has changed, he goes and does something even more terrible. I'm just going to keep away from him as much as possible."

"Well, I think he sounds awesome," Māui said. "He can hang out with me and Atlas. Maybe Mars too. And Hades. You can stay in your room if you like; the rest of us boys are gonna have a blast."

"Well," Mum said, frowning. "I must get on. There's so much to do, and I need to make up a room for our new arrival! I think I'll put him in Room 16. It has a lovely view."

"We can do that," Māui said straight away. "Atlas and I would love to help, wouldn't we, Atlas?"

"We would?" Atlas replied, confused. Māui had never shown any signs of being helpful before.

Māui kicked him under the table. "Yes. We. Would," he said.

Atlas shrugged. "OK, sure," he agreed.

"Thank you, boys." Mum smiled.

"I'm going to go and look through some Nordic cookbooks," Dad said, heading off towards the kitchen.

"We'll get started on the decorations,"

Venus said. "Come on, Ari, we can hang out some bunting."

"Oh, speaking of decorations . . ." Hades produced a rolled-up piece of fabric. "I made another wall hanging." He unfurled it for them to see. It read:

LIVE.
LAUGH.
LOVE.
DIE.

Atlas frowned. He wasn't entirely sure Hades was getting the tone right with his inspirational quotes, but at least he was trying.

"Do you like it?" Hades asked brightly as he hung it on the dining room wall.

"Yes, it's very . . . thought-provoking," Atlas replied politely.

Once they'd finished their food, he and Māui headed off towards the staircase to the bedrooms, leaving Thor alone, staring at his plate.

"What's going on?" Atlas asked Māui as they entered the room that Loki would be staying in. "Are you planning some kind of surprise for our new guest?"

Māui looked offended. "Do you really think so little of me that you believe I'd play a dastardly trick on an honoured guest at our humble hotel?"

"Yes," Atlas said, flatly.

"I'm hurt," Māui said.

The two of them proceeded to fix the room, putting new sheets on the bed and dusting the surfaces. Atlas plumped the pillows while Māui stocked the mini fridge. Māui insisted they do a thorough job and after half an hour, the room looked and smelled wonderful. As they were leaving, Atlas said, "OK, so I guess I misjudged you. I apologise."

"Thank you," Māui replied. "Apology accepted." Then he clicked his fingers and suddenly Atlas's insides felt like they'd turned inside out. His head spinning, he turned back and blinked in astonishment.

Every last bit of furniture in the room was now on the ceiling. The room had been turned completely *UPSIDE DOWN*.

"Hope Loki can fly," Māui said. "Otherwise he won't be able to get into bed."

"What have you done?!" Atlas cried.

"Your mum asked us to fix up his room," Māui said. "Well, I've FIXED it, and now everything's UP."

Atlas laughed. Spending time with Māui

was never boring. And he suspected when Loki arrived, things were going to get even more interesting . . .

CHAPTER
FOUR

"**A** bit higher!" said Thor.

"What's going on?" Hades asked, entering the lobby. It was a hive of activity. He joined Atlas and Māui, who were each holding one end of a banner that read:

WELCOME, LOKI!

"We're getting ready for Loki's arrival," Atlas explained as they hung up the banner.

"Thor looks . . . different," Hades said.

"He's been in the salon," Venus explained from behind them. "He didn't want Loki to think he'd aged."

"He's two thousand years old," Hades pointed out.

"That reminds me," Venus said. "I need to reorder some concealer. Thor used it all up."

"Someone sweep the floor," Thor roared at them.

"On it," Mars said. Atlas was surprised to see Mars take orders from Thor, who was usually his rival. But then again he'd

never seen Thor
so organised. The
thunder god was
ordering everyone
about like he was
Odin himself.

"Quetzalcóatl!"
Thor snapped. "Take
that barbecue outside, please."

"Sorry," Quetzalcóatl said, picking up an
enormous brazier and heading for the door.

"What are you cooking, dude?" Māui asked
him.

"Ears."

"I'm sorry, what?" Atlas asked in alarm.

"Of corn," Quetzalcóatl explained.

Bastet, in her human form, was lounging on a sunny reading ledge at the window, looking out into the garden. Even when the Egyptian cat goddess was a human, she exhibited feline qualities and spent most of her time at rest.

"Bastet!" Thor snapped. She turned her head slowly to look at him.

"Having a nice, relaxing time?" Thor asked sarcastically.

"Yes, thank you," Bastet replied, then yawned.

"Can I remind you that Loki will be arriving soon, and I want to make a good

impression. Otherwise he will certainly
tell Odin and then who knows what might
happen?"

"It's important to YOU to make a good
impression," she corrected. "I don't care. And
anyway, it's too late."

"Why?" Thor asked, fuming.

"Because Odin has just arrived."

The great double doors of the Hotel of the
Gods slammed open and everyone turned to
stare. With a great FANFARE OF TRUMPETS
and a BRIGHT FLASH OF LIGHT, someone
came flying down from the sky, riding a huge
stallion. Atlas saw to his astonishment that
the horse had eight legs.

"Sleipnir," he gasped. It was Odin's steed.

The great horse came clattering down on to the polished marble floor of the lobby and the huge, shaggy figure on its back leapt off and stood, legs apart, glaring around at them all with his one, bright eye.

"**FATHER**!" Thor spluttered, somehow managing to go bright red and completely white at the same time. "**I wasn't expecting. I mean, we didn't—**"

"**Of course you didn't**," Odin roared. "**Because you are a fool!**"

Atlas felt his heart thump like a rabbit's foot. He'd heard them all talk about how terrifying Odin was, but nothing could have prepared him for the sheer awesome presence of the king of the Viking gods. Atlas, Māui and Hades quietly backed away into the shadows. Even Mars looked nervous and Bastet, in her cat form, had shot out of an open window.

Odin looked around at the decorations in the lobby. His gaze fell upon Quetzalcóatl, smiling and holding a platter of barbecued corn. "What is this? A children's birthday party?"

"It . . . it is to welcome my old friend Loki," Thor stammered.

"Loki is a great warrior, a wise leader, a brilliant Scrabble player," Odin boomed. "He deserves better than a bit of bunting and a piece of burnt sweetcorn."

"Rude," Quetzalcóatl muttered under his breath.

"You have been neglecting your duties in Asgard," Odin roared at Thor. "You are lazy; you spend all your time here on permanent vacation while Loki works hard, winning glory and improving his mind through study, self-reflection and wordsearches."

"Forgive me, Father!" Thor moaned, nearly in tears.

"Prostrate yourself when you ask me for forgiveness!" Odin roared.

Thor dropped to his knees, then lay flat

on the floor. **"FORGIVE ME, OH GREAT ODIN,"** he wailed, now sobbing uncontrollably. Odin regarded him thoughtfully. The assembled crowd watched silently.

"I may forgive you if you admit that you are a **great blond buffoon**," Odin said.

"I am a **great blond buffoon**," Thor said.

"You are lower than a sandworm."

"I am **lower than a sandworm.**"

"And **uglier than a cave goblin.**"

"And **uglier than a cave goblin**," Thor repeated.

"And **dumber than a box of rocks**."

"I am **dumber than a box of rocks**," Thor said, snivelling.

"And Loki is much cleverer and more handsome and princely than you."

"And Loki is much . . . wait," Thor said. He looked up from the floor at Odin, a dawning look of horror in his eyes.

Odin had disappeared. In his place was a dark-haired, slim figure with icy blue eyes and a devilish grin.

"**LOKI**!" Thor cried.

Loki held up his arms.

"**Surprise**!" The assembled gods laughed at the trick. Thor got to his feet, grabbed his hammer and stomped off in utter humiliation.

"Where are you going, bro?" Loki called after him. "I'd hoped we might be able to catch up!"

Thor stopped dead, spun on his heels and roared, "**I AM NOT YOUR BROTHER**!" Then he turned back and stormed off.

"A shape-shifter!" Māui muttered. "Well played, Loki, my man."

"I saw through the disguise, of course," Hades said. "I can see right into the soul of any man or god."

"Right," said Māui, rolling his eyes. Hades wandered off and Atlas and Māui walked up to Loki and introduced themselves.

"That was some trick you pulled," Māui said. "Most impressive, dude."

"I'm not sure Thor saw the funny side of it though," Atlas added. He felt bad for Thor. The thunder god could sometimes be unintentionally quite dangerous, hurling his hammer about the place, but he'd always been kind and generous. As funny as Loki's trick had been, a part of Atlas hated to see pranks that made other people feel bad.

"Thor never could take a joke," Loki said airily. "He always sulks. It might take him a day or two to get over it."

"You can hang with me and Atlas instead," Māui said with a twinkle in his eye. "But first we'll show you to your room."

"Thank you," Loki said with a little bow. "That would be most kind."

They headed up the stairs. Atlas could tell Māui was trying not to laugh.

"It's ages since I've had a proper holiday," Loki said.

"There's tons to do here," Atlas explained enthusiastically. "There's swimming, tennis, biking, horse riding and archery. My dad does the food and he can cook anything you like."

They reached Loki's room. Number 16.

"After you," Māui said, opening the door and waving Loki in. The god entered. Māui and Atlas looked at each other, stifling giggles. They waited a few moments, then they followed Loki through the doorway.

The boys stopped still in astonishment. Loki was sitting calmly in a plush armchair,

upside down, on the ceiling. He winked at them.

The next thing Atlas knew was that he was falling. UPWARDS. Gravity had been reversed!

With a huge thump, Atlas hit the ceiling, which was now the floor.

OOF! Māui landed on top of him.

Atlas groaned. Then he looked out of the window and saw a bird fly past, upside down.

"Never try to trick the trickster god," Loki said, smiling wickedly. He looked around the room and nodded. "I think I'm going to like it here."

★ ★ CHAPTER ★ ★
FIVE

The next morning, gravity back to normal, Atlas and Māui were in the kitchen sipping Dad's special Ambrosia smoothies. Thor was in there too, lurking near the great fireplace, hiding from Loki. Dad was working on the menu for the special **MIDSUMMER'S NIGHT FEAST.** He was very excited. He kept pestering Atlas's mum for historical information on the Vikings.

Mum, who was something of an expert on mythology, was doing her best to help, whilst struggling with a mountain of washing up from breakfast.

"I need to know what they ate," Dad asked. "It has to be authentic."

"I don't know," Mum replied, looking harassed. "Lots of fish, I suppose. Salmon, cod."

"Fish and chips?" Dad exclaimed in dismay. For many years Atlas's dad had run a fish and chip shop, and he didn't look thrilled at the thought of going back to that.

"Well, I don't think they had deep-fat

fryers," Mum replied. "Or mushy peas. So probably not. They would have pickled their fish. Herring in particular."

"Pickled herring?" Dad said, looking doubtful. Then he shrugged and picked up a cookbook and flipped through a few pages. "Here is a recipe," he exclaimed after a while. "First, catch your fish . . ."

"**Fishing!**" Thor cried from across the room. "**An excellent idea.** I haven't been fishing in years. I will catch all the fish you need. It will be a good way for me to get away from—"

But Thor was interrupted by the door bursting open. Loki strode in, grinning wolfishly.

"Did someone mention fishing?" he asked. "Sounds great. I once spent a year living as a fish. It made me something of an expert on catching them."

Thor groaned.

"It will be a good opportunity for us to catch up, bro," Loki went on.

"Not your brother," Thor muttered.

"Can Atlas and I come?" Māui asked. "I'm something of a fisherman myself."

"Sure!" Loki said. Apparently it was his trip now.

"What about you, Hades?" Atlas asked.

Hades shook his head. "Fishing isn't my thing," he explained. "Fish don't go to hell. Not even the really naughty ones. Also, the seas and rivers in hell are always on fire."

And so, after breakfast, the four of them left the hotel grounds and followed a winding path between a couple of mountains.

After quite some time, Atlas thought he heard a seagull calling and he caught the faint whiff of salt.

"Ah, the sea!" Māui cried, breathing it in. "How I have missed you. Those fish aren't going to know what hit them."

"Is that how you catch fish in Hawai'i?" Loki asked. "By hitting them?"

"You'll see," Māui said with a wink. "Hey, Hades told me a joke. What do you call a fish with no eyes? A fsh."

Atlas chuckled politely, but Loki only sighed.

"Don't you like jokes, Loki?" Māui asked.

"I enjoy funny jokes," Loki replied.

The group came to the top of a cliff. Far below lay a sheltered cove with a pebble beach. A steep, winding path led down to the cove. They carefully made their way along it.

"What do you give a fish with hearing

difficulties?" Māui asked. "A herring aid."

This time even Atlas couldn't raise a laugh, and Māui resorted to a grumpy silence. Māui was even worse at telling jokes than Hades, it seemed.

At the bottom of the cliff, there was a Viking longboat resting at anchor. Atlas could read the name on the stern. "**EYE OF THE STORM**."

"This is Odin's longboat," Thor said as they clambered aboard. "Does he know you've taken it?"

"He won't mind," Loki said. "Probably."

Loki handed Atlas an oar. Atlas looked at him blankly.

"You need to row," Loki explained. "No wind today."

Rowing, it turned out, was hard work. After a few failed attempts, in which they found themselves going round in circles, they finally worked out that they needed Thor rowing on one side of the boat and the other three rowing on the other, because Thor was so much stronger than the rest of them.

Even then he had to row one-handed. Atlas shook his head and wondered just why Loki was prepared to play so many tricks on Thor. One blow from those mighty fists, and goodbye Loki.

"Of course, I invented the fish-hook," Māui puffed as they hauled away. "I've used my magic hook for all sorts of things – slowing down the sun, dragging the islands of Hawai'i from the seabed. They even named a constellation after my hook."

"Shame you never caught any fish with it," Loki said.

Māui blinked at him, stung.

"And anyway," Loki went on, "you didn't invent it. Your grandma gave it to you."

Māui's mouth dropped open in dismay.

"I, on the other hand," boasted Loki, "invented the fishing net. Much better at bringing in a big haul."

"It was a foolish thing to do," Thor muttered. "Since you spent a year disguised as a fish. Why invent the very thing most likely to catch you?"

Māui laughed.

Loki shrugged and held his fist to his chest in a poetic manner. "We are all ultimately hurt by the things we create."

Then he farted. "See?" PARP!

"I don't need your hooks or your nets," Thor grumbled.

"Then what are you going to use?" Atlas asked gently.

Thor grinned. "The same thing I use for everything else," he said, and held up his hammer.

Māui sighed.

"Perhaps a wager is in order," Loki said. "Whichever of us catches the most fish, by weight, is the winner and will take the prize."

"Fine," Thor said.

"You're on, dude," Māui added.

Atlas just shrugged.

Once they'd reached a point where they all
agreed there were likely to be lots of fish, they
cast their lines, or at least Atlas and Māui did.
Thor knelt in the prow, staring down into the
water and waving his hammer threateningly.

"Gonna catch the biggest fish," he
muttered to himself. "Then **POW**, gonna
bonk it on the head. And win this bet. Wipe
the smile off that dummy's stupid face. Then
I'm gonna eat a sandwich."

Loki, on the other hand, stretched out at
the back of the boat and seemed to nod off to
sleep in the warm sunshine.

Atlas sighed happily. He didn't really
care about the contest, and didn't even

particularly want to catch any fish, pickled or otherwise. He was just happy to be with his friends in the sunshine. Māui prattled away, telling stories about his fishing exploits with his brothers in the olden days. After a while Atlas found himself growing drowsy. His eyelids drooped and his head dropped on to his chest . . .

He woke with a start as something tugged on his line. He began reeling it in.

"I've got one!" he cried. "I've got one." And indeed he had. He jerked the rod up, and there on the end of his line was a fish, wriggling away, shining in the sunlight.

It was a little on the small side.

Thor snorted. "Call that a fish?" he said. "It's a minnow at best."

Atlas shrugged. It did look quite small, but that wasn't the point. He'd caught a fish! He popped it off the hook, apologised to it and threw it back into the sea with a *PLOP*.

The boat grew quiet, and Atlas was nearly dropping off again when—

SPLASH!

A spray of cold water hit Atlas in the face. There was something in the water! Something big!

"I've got one, I've got one!" Māui cried. "My hook has done it again!"

Atlas and Thor rushed over to help with

the tussle. The fish was enormous! They could see it thrashing in the water as it struggled against the big, glowing hook. Māui's muscled arms were taut and his jaw clenched as he fought to reel in the powerful creature.

Eventually, with the help of Thor and Atlas (mostly Thor, to be fair) they brought the fish aboard. It was the size of a calf, and its scales shone bright gold and silver. Māui gasped as Thor lifted it, cradling it in his great arms.

"Look at this, Loki!" Māui cried in triumph, eyes searching the deck. "Loki? Where is he?"

Atlas looked around, puzzled. Loki was gone. But then Thor spoke.

"Oh no," he said.

Atlas turned back to see a look of dawning realisation on Thor's face. He was staring

down at the fish cradled in his arms. It thrashed its tail, stretched up and planted a big kiss on Thor's lips.

Then the fish turned back into Loki.

SMACK!

"How safe I feel, cradled in your arms, my dear brother," Loki cried, passionately. "I always knew you loved me . . ."

Thor dropped him unceremoniously on the deck. "You're NOT my brother," he growled, then stormed off with a disgusted look.

Loki grinned, then pulled out his fishing net and flung it into the sea. He hauled it back up almost instantly and Atlas was astonished to see it was absolutely stuffed with fish.

"**Ah, herring!**" Loki shouted. "**My favourite!**"

"Oh wow!" Atlas exclaimed. "What a haul!

That's brilliant, Loki!"

Māui yanked Atlas away. "Whose side are you on?" he hissed.

"Sorry, Māui," Atlas said. "But maybe we should all try to get on. You know, stop having contests and playing tricks on each other and just . . . you know, hang?"

"We might as well go back now," Loki said breezily as he dumped the fish on the deck.

"Go back?" Thor cried. "But I haven't got into my stride yet."

"Me neither," Māui protested. "I just need to get into the rhythm. I'm going to get a huge one, you'll see!"

"We have all the fish we need for pickling,"

Loki said. "This will take Atlas's dad days to prepare."

"You would say that," Thor growled. "Just when you happen to be ahead in the contest."

"Don't worry," Loki said. "We'll forget the contest. We'll tell everyone back at the hotel that we caught the fish together. There's plenty to go around."

"See?" Atlas hissed to Māui. "Loki isn't a bad guy. We can all get on."

Thor and Māui looked at Loki doubtfully.

"Though of course the four of us will know the truth," Loki went on with a cheeky grin. **"That I am the best fisherman of all!"**

CHAPTER SIX

Thor roared in anger and hefted his hammer, but Loki just raised a finger and a gust of wind caught the sail. The longboat lurched, and Thor fell over in surprise and crashed to the deck. They went scudding across the waves towards home.

"Looks like I'm the better sailor too," Loki said, winking. He was now wearing a pirate's hat at a jaunty angle. He also had a parrot on his shoulder and a tattoo of an anchor on his arm. Atlas shook his head. Loki wasn't going to win over his friends with this attitude.

There was little conversation on the return journey. Māui and Thor sat at the back, glowering. Loki sat in the middle, counting fish loudly. Atlas sat at the front, enjoying the spray of the sea and the screaming of the seabirds that hovered around the boat, eyeing up Loki's catch.

When they got to the jetty, Loki turned to Thor and Māui. "Tell you what," he said. "If you help me carry this lot back to the hotel, I'll give you each a share of my haul."

They looked doubtful, but Atlas stepped forward. "That's a kind gesture," he said. "Thank you, Loki."

"You're welcome," Loki said. "You boys know that I like to tease. But it's just a bit of fun. I really do think we can all be friends."

Māui and Thor looked at each other and shrugged.

"OK," they said sullenly.

Thor carried the net up the steps. Even with his great strength it was hard work.

Then Māui carried the haul across the fields, back to the hotel.

"I'll do the last bit," Loki said breezily when they reached the front gates. He

snatched the net from Māui and trotted into
the lobby, where he dumped the fish all over
the shiny marble floor.

"**Behold my haul**," he cried. The assembled
gods and goddesses clapped and cheered.
The fish slipped and slid. Bastet appeared as
if from nowhere, her nostrils flared and her

eyes wide with delight.

"Wait," Thor puffed as he followed Loki into the lobby.

"What about our shares?" Māui added, staggering in.

"Of course," Loki said. He reached into his pocket and pulled out two tiny fish. "These magnificent specimens were caught by my good friends here," he said, then tossed the tiddlers on to the pile. The other gods roared with laughter and Atlas winced to see Thor and Māui looking so embarrassed.

"What a wonderful catch!" Atlas's dad cried. "I will prepare my pickling pots immediately. This **MIDSUMMER'S NIGHT**

CELEBRATION will be spectacular!"

"I really hate that guy," Māui said, scowling as the other gods and goddesses clapped Loki on the back, congratulating him on his success. Bastet sniffed the fish, a dreamy look on her face.

"Now do you see what I've been saying?" Thor asked. "I tried to warn you, but no, you were all, 'Oh, Loki's a legend! It'll be nice to have a new face around here. Let's invite the new guy into the gang.'"

"Don't worry about it," Atlas said. "I know you're both really good at fishing too. You just didn't have any luck today."

"Great," Thor muttered. "Now I'm being

patronised by a mortal kid."

"A mortal who actually caught a fish," Māui reminded him.

Thor grunted and gripped his hammer tightly.

"Maybe it's time to give Thor some space," Atlas said to Māui, quickly leading him away.

"What is that stink?" Hades said as he wandered into the kitchen a few days later. "It smells like a harpy's fart."

"Dad's pickling the herring," Atlas explained. "It's going to be delicious."

"As long as Loki keeps out of my kitchen," Dad said, grumpily. "He swapped my sugar and salt yesterday and I accidentally invented sweet and salty herring. Zero out of ten, would not recommend."

"Luckily you still have about a million fish left," Mum said, wandering past with a box full of glass preserving jars. "We've pickled so many herring I'm running out of places to store these."

Atlas wandered through the dining room and out on to the patio. Midsummer's Eve was fast approaching, and the hotel was abuzz with activity. Ari was helping Venus decorate the patio with bunting and lights. The garden doors were open wide in the warm afternoon. Butterflies and bees flittered from flower to flower and Hades, with help from his demons, was busy constructing a long table for the feast.

Thor popped his head out of a window.

"Is he here?" the thunder god asked in a whisper.

"Who?" Venus whispered back.

"Loki," Thor hissed.

"Nope, haven't seen him," Venus replied, then stretched up to hang another length of bunting.

"I saw him by the pool earlier," Hades said,

"taunting the water dragon."

Thor's head disappeared, then a moment later he came outside. Atlas saw he was carrying an axe instead of his hammer.

"Right, I'm off to the woods to cut logs for the bonfire," he said. "Don't tell him where I've gone."

"Can I come with you?" Atlas asked. "Cerbie needs a walk."

"Of course!" Thor said.

They set off towards the woodlands, which bordered the grounds of the hotel. Cerbie ran ahead as they walked through the trees.

Thor stopped by a massive fallen oak. It looked as if it had been lying there for years.

"Properly seasoned," Thor explained. "No need to cut down living trees. Dead ones burn so much better."

Atlas watched in awe as Thor began to chop, great swings of the axe cutting deep into the hard wood.

"The bonfire will ward off evil spirits and encourage a good harvest," Thor said as he chopped, puffing only slightly.

"Is Midsummer a big deal then?" Atlas asked. His family hadn't lived at the hotel last summer, so he didn't know what to expect.

"It's our MOST important celebration," Thor said. **"All Vikings love Midsummer. Except Odin."**

"Why's that?" Atlas asked as the axe came
whipping down again and Thor threw
another half dozen logs on to the pile.

"He's allergic to pickled herring," Thor said.

Once he thought the pile was big enough,
Thor threw the logs into three huge sacks

and one small one which Atlas was able to carry. Before they left, Thor picked up a long thin trunk, trimmed off the branches and balanced it carefully on his shoulder.

"What's that for?" Atlas asked

"You'll see," Thor said with a wink. Then he strode off through the trees, Atlas and Cerbie struggling to keep up.

Upon their arrival back at the hotel, Cerbie ran inside to eat his dinner. Thor dumped the bags of logs, then he took the tree trunk and jammed one end hard into the ground.

"What a fantastic maypole!" Venus cried. "*Well done, Thor*!"

"And so much firewood," Hades said with

a grin. "This year's bonfire will burn hotter than, well, hell!"

Bastet rubbed her back against the pole, purring happily.

Even Quetzalcóatl had come out and clapped Thor on the back. "The maypole still needs ribbons. Allow me to assist." Quetzalcóatl muttered some words, waved his hands and Atlas gasped as three long snakes sprouted from the ground around the pole and coiled their way up the pole to the top.

As everyone watched the snakes writhing around the maypole, Atlas caught a glimpse of Loki at the back of the crowd. He did not look happy at the attention Thor was getting.

To Atlas's surprise, the trickster suddenly transformed. He grew larger and larger, spouting black hair all over his body. His hands became paws and he dropped down on to all fours, still growing. His features changed, his nose becoming a snout and huge teeth springing from his jaws. Finally, two more heads popped from his neck.

To Atlas's horror, Loki had transformed into Cerberus – the savage, three-headed hellhound. Atlas looked around for the real Cerbie, but his little dog was nowhere to be seen. He had to warn the others!

"I'm really not sure about the snakes," Venus said to Quetzalcóatl. "Perhaps we should just use ribbons."

"I can make them different colours if you like," Quetzalcóatl replied.

"It's not so much the colour," Venus said, tactfully. "It's more the spitting venom and sharp fangs."

"Look out!" cried Atlas. But his warning was drowned out by a three-throated **ROAR!**

Growling and snarling, Cerberus ran towards Bastet. The cat goddess sprang up the pole, yowling in fear. The huge hellhound raced around the base of it, barking and snapping furiously. The snakes at the top of the pole hissed at Bastet, who batted their heads away with her paws.

"*Stop*!" Venus cried. "*Quetzalcóatl, don't let your snakes bite Bastet*!"

"They probably won't," Quetzalcóatl said, looking up.

"*Somebody do something*!" screamed Venus.

"Don't be frightened, my darling," said Mars, throwing his arms around her. "I will protect you."

Luckily, Thor came to the rescue. He plucked up Māui and stood him on his own shoulders. Then he grabbed Atlas and effortlessly threw him up in the air. Māui grabbed Atlas and perched him, in turn, upon his own shoulders. As the tower of

bodies swayed precariously, Atlas reached up and Bastet hopped into his arms, purring in relief.

Meanwhile, each of Cerberus's three mouths had gleefully seized the tail of a snake. As the hellhound ran around the maypole, the snakes wrapped around Thor, Māui, and Atlas, pressing them tightly against the maypole. Atlas could feel the snakes squeezing him so tightly he could barely breathe.

"**What sorcery made these serpents**?!" Thor exclaimed. "**I cannot break them.**"

Venus whacked Quetzalcóatl on his arm. "*Lose the snakes!*" she ordered him. "*NOW!*"

Quetzalcóatl sighed, but snapped his fingers, magically dissolving the snakes. With the sudden release, Atlas, Māui and Thor came tumbling to the ground. Bastet streaked across the lawn, hissing furiously.

"Waste of three perfectly good snakes," Quetzalcóatl muttered. "They don't grow on trees, you know."

Just then, Atlas heard a noise and turned to see Cerbie come scampering across the grass, his tail wagging. There was a smudge of dog food on his nose.

"NOW you show up," Atlas said. He looked around, hoping to demonstrate to everyone that Cerbie and Cerberus were two very different dogs. However, the large hellhound had disappeared. There was no sign of Loki, either.

"Your dog has been causing mayhem," Venus said, glaring at Atlas.

"It wasn't Cerbie," Atlas said. "It was Loki."

"We all saw him," Bastet snapped at Atlas, back in her human form. "And Loki isn't even here."

"But . . ." Atlas began.

"**SILENCE, MORTAL!**" Quetzalcóatl roared. "I have lost three snakes thanks to your mischievous hound. If he cannot be controlled, then he must be confined."

"**No!**" Atlas cried. But it was no good. The

gods wouldn't listen.

Hades came over and clipped a lead on to Cerbie, who stood, tail drooping. "Maybe he should stay downstairs with me for a while. They'll forget about it in a couple of days."

And so Atlas watched, his heart breaking, as poor Cerbie was led away, back down the stairs to the basement.

★ ★ CHAPTER ★ ★

SEVEN

Atlas barely slept that night. He missed having Cerbie at the end of his bed, even though the dog always farted in his sleep.

After breakfast, he went outside and found Thor stacking firewood along with Māui. They were preparing the bonfire for the big celebration. But Atlas didn't feel excited about it any more.

"What's wrong?" Māui asked.

"I miss Cerbie," said Atlas glumly. "It's so unfair. I tried to tell them it was Loki, but they wouldn't listen."

"I warned you about Loki. He's a pain in the neck," said Thor.

"Oh no," said Māui. "Speak of the devil."

Loki strolled up the path towards them. "Hey, guys. Hope you didn't mind my little prank the other day," he said, grinning. "It was just a bit of fun. Look, let me help with the bonfire to make it up to you."

"We don't need your help," Thor said through gritted teeth.

"I insist," Loki cried. "After all, it was me

107

who brought fire to humans in the first place. Banishing the darkness."

"Excuse me?" Māui said.

"You're excused," Loki replied.

"I am the fire god," Māui said hotly.

"Demigod," said Loki.

"I think you'll find that I gave fire to humans," Māui said, ignoring his rival's interruption. "My grandmother had fire which she kept in her fingernails. She used to let us have some from time to time. But I thought, why shouldn't we have our own fire? Both gods and humans? She was being selfish. So I tricked her into pulling out all her fingernails and giving them to me."

There was a silence. Everyone stopped stacking logs and looked at Māui.

"That's revolting," Thor said eventually. "You made an old lady pull out all her fingernails?"

Māui shrugged guiltily. "They grew back."

"It's still a horrible thing to do," Atlas said.

"Different times," Māui said vaguely. "Anyway, the point is that some of the sparks got caught in the wood of the kaikōmako tree and from then on people could just use those trees to make fires, and no one had to ask anyone else's permission and no one had to lose any more fingernails."

"What about you, Loki?" Atlas asked.

"How did you give fire to humans?"

Loki shrugged. "I didn't torture my gran, that's for sure. There was plenty of fire in Asgard. I just took some to Earth and gave it to the first human I saw. Odin was furious, of course."

"Did he punish you?" Atlas asked.

"Nope," Loki said. "I blamed a human. Totally got away with it."

"What a surprise," Thor said, sighing.

"Anyway," Loki went on. "Maybe we need to settle the question, who is the real god of fire, with a little contest?" He looked at Māui.

"Oh, no, now come on . . ." Atlas began. "No more contests; can't we all just get along—"

"**You're on**," Māui interrupted, narrowing his eyes.

Atlas sighed. *Here we go again . . .*

Loki took a few steps back, then blasted a small fireball at Māui, who blocked it easily. It faded away in a puff of smoke.

Māui laughed. "**Is that the best you can do?**" he sneered, then he let rip with a massive stream of fire from his outstretched fingertips. The fire blasted towards Loki, who . . . disappeared.

"**Uh-oh**!" Atlas gasped.

The fireball shot across the lawn, setting fire to dozens of wooden deckchairs and Hades' table before finally reaching the maypole, which was immediately set ablaze. As it burned, it shot bright red sparks up into the sky.

"Māui!" Venus screamed.

"Oh no," Māui said. He rushed over to try and help. But it was Ari who came sprinting out with a fire extinguisher and put out the blazes. Unfortunately, the maypole couldn't be saved. It was left as a blackened stick of wood, which snapped and crumbled into black dust as they stood and watched.

"Atlas!" Ari snapped. "Look what you've done! First your dog, now this?"

"It wasn't me!" Atlas cried, knowing he sounded pathetic.

Ari stormed off, clearly furious with him.

Loki's peals of laughter could be heard throughout the garden.

"**I really, really hate that guy,**" Thor said.

The fuming Māui clenched his fists. "There's only room for one trickster god at the Hotel of the Gods," he growled. "And I was here first."

Loki's voice floated over from somewhere in the darkness. **"May the best trickster win."**

Māui turned, clenched his fists and roared, **"CHALLENGE ACCEPTED!"**

CHAPTER
EIGHT

"**A** water bucket on a door jamb?" Atlas suggested.

"**Dumb**," Māui replied as he paced back and forth.

"Cling film over the toilet bowl?"

"**Childish**," Māui tutted.

"Knock down ginger?" Atlas said, racking his brains for more pranks, jokes or tricks.

"What's knock down ginger?" Māui asked, looking at Atlas with interest.

"When you knock at a door and run off before they answer."

Māui stared at Atlas and shook his head. **"Not cool, little dude. You humans are just so, so unimaginative."** The boys were in Māui's Tiki-themed room, with coconuts and palm trees and a little smoothie bar. They were trying to come up with ideas for pranking Loki, but so far Māui had pooh-poohed all Atlas's best ideas. Atlas wasn't entirely sure he wanted to get involved in the contest, but he thought he might be able to stop Māui from getting too carried away.

"When you hear about some of the tricks I pulled," Māui was saying, "hoo boy."

"Like what?" Atlas asked.

"Like . . . err, well, once I used my fish-hook to slow down the sun."

"Why?"

"It was going too fast, man," Māui cried. "Not enough sunshine in the day. A dude needs time to bake if he wants a killer tan."

"So, what other tricks did you pull?" Atlas asked.

"Did you know birds used to be invisible?" Māui asked.

"What? No!"

"I made them visible to everyone. Pretty

cool, huh?" said Māui.

"OK, but that's not really a trick."

"I could make them invisible again?"

Atlas shook his head.

There was silence for a while as the two of them tried to think of the perfect trick to pull on Loki.

"I'm good at voices," Māui said suddenly.

"What?" Atlas asked. "Oh, err, like who?"

Māui thought. "I can do my dad? I mimicked his voice when I tricked my way into hell."

"Right," Atlas said.

"Māui, **CLEAN YOUR ROOM!**" Māui roared in a deep voice. "See?"

"Firstly, no one knows your dad," Atlas said. "And secondly, if we wanted to go to hell, we don't need to trick our way in. We could just ask Hades to open the fire door in his basement." Atlas felt a pang as he thought about Cerbie down in the basement.

"Hmm," Māui said, then resumed his thoughtful pacing. After a while, he stopped and held up a finger. "You know, I created just about every Pacific island," he said. "I could drag something up from the sea?"

"Again, not a trick," Atlas said. "Your feats are impressive but I think we need to trick Loki into doing something. Something that will get him in trouble. But not too much trouble," he added, as he saw the gleam in Māui's eyes.

They were interrupted by a roar from down the hall. Rushing off to see what was going on, Atlas found Thor in the lobby, looking miserable. Mum had put her arm around his shoulders (she had to go up on her tiptoes) and was saying, "There, there, dear."

"What's wrong?" Atlas asked, concerned.

"My hammer has been stolen!" Thor cried. He fell to his knees. **"Mjölnir, where are you**?!"

"Where's the last place you saw it?" Mum asked gently. "Let's retrace your steps."

Mum, Atlas and Ari helped Thor hunt for his hammer. First they went to the gym. "I was working on my abs," Thor said, lifting up his shirt to show off his tummy muscles.

"Wow!" said Mum. "That's very impressive."

Thor's six pack was on display, but his hammer was nowhere to be seen.

"Where were you before the gym?" Mum asked.

"The salon," Thor said. "I can't remember

why I was there, though."

"I think you were getting a spray tan," Ari said. Thor glared at her.

They searched the salon. Thor's method of looking for things was to pick up every object or item of furniture and hurl it behind him to see what was underneath. It was dangerous, but effective. It soon became clear that the hammer was not in the salon.

"Can we get some help here?" Atlas called over to Hermes, who was reading a magazine while Venus gave him a pedicure.

The messenger god whipped around the hotel, rounding up as many gods and goddesses as possible. They assembled in the lobby. Unsurprisingly, Loki hadn't bothered to show up.

"OK, everyone," Atlas shouted. "Mjölnir is missing. And there's a reward for finding it."

"What's the reward?" Māui asked eagerly.

"**Twenty jars of pickled herring**!" Dad cried.

"Make it forty!" Mum said as she tried to cram more jars into the cupboard under the winding staircase.

And so began a massive, hotel-wide search for the hammer. Everyone split up, with Māui and Quetzalcóatl heading outside to search the stables and pool area. Mars and Venus checked the bedrooms. Hades checked the underworld. Even Bastet was persuaded to help. "After all," Mum said, "you know every hidey-hole and secret passage in this hotel."

Atlas checked in the kitchen, where the scent of brine made his eyes water. He looked in every cupboard and storeroom, most of which were filled with jars of pickled herring. Above him, he could hear the crash and smash of Thor tearing the hotel apart trying to find Mjölnir.

And then . . .

"**FOUND IT**!" someone cried from somewhere upstairs.

Running out of the kitchen, Atlas followed the other gods and goddesses, who were hurrying upstairs – to Māui's room. He squeezed his way through the crush and saw Loki pointing to the handle of Thor's hammer sticking out from under Māui's bed.

Atlas was sure it hadn't been there before. He would have noticed it. He'd been in there with Māui when the hammer went missing.

"I guess this is one of your famous pranks, Māui," said Loki.

Atlas frowned. Loki hadn't even been part of the search party. How did he even know the hammer was missing?

Thor glowered at Māui.

"It wasn't me," Māui spluttered, looking astonished. "Honest!"

Atlas saw a sly grin spread across Loki's face.

"Did you put it there, Loki?" Atlas asked suspiciously.

All eyes turned to the Viking trickster. A look of hurt innocence came over Loki's face.

"Me?" he asked, a hand on his chest. "It couldn't have been me. I cannot even lift Thor's hammer, see?" He reached down and grabbed the handle, which didn't move an inch. Loki grunted with the effort but Mjölnir didn't budge.

"I am not worthy," Loki said, eyes wide with innocence.

"I . . . I . . ." Māui stuttered as Thor's face went from red to purple. "I can't lift it either."

Thor bent and picked up the hammer, then tossed it lightly to Māui, who instinctively caught it by the handle. Then, realising what he'd just done, he dropped it guiltily. It landed on his own toe with a crunch. He howled in pain. Before Atlas could say anything, Thor grabbed poor Māui, dragged him over to the window and hurled

him out like a rag doll.

Atlas watched in dismay as his friend sailed out of sight, landing somewhere in the woods. Then Thor took his hammer and stomped out of the room.

"Show's over," Mum said, shooing the gods and goddesses out of Māui's room.

"I'd better go and get the prize," said Dad.

Loki was the last to leave. He patted Atlas on the shoulder as he went and leaned in close. "Tell your friend Māui it's one-nil to me," he whispered, winking.

Atlas's eyes widened in indignation. Once again, someone else was taking the blame for Loki's mischief.

CHAPTER NINE

The next day Hades brought Cerbie back upstairs. Atlas was delighted. This was the first good thing that had happened for ages. It almost made up for the fact that Māui had barely left his room since Thor threw him out of the window.

Around mid-morning, Venus sent Atlas and Thor to the garden with instructions to gather flowers for the Midsummer's Night Celebration.

"Venus said she's making wreaths for everyone," Atlas said, trying to make conversation. He snipped off a red poppy. "She says flowers are a symbol of new life."

Thor just grunted as he plucked a poppy with his bare hand. It seemed that picking flowers wasn't really his thing. Tearing up trees? Perhaps. Defeating an army of Ice Giants? Maybe. But picking poppies? Not so much.

And neither, apparently, was conversation.

Atlas sighed. He wished Māui had come with them. He missed his friend. *At least*

Cerbie is back, he thought, watching the dog race around the garden. Atlas checked his pocket to make sure he had plenty of poo bags.

Once they had enough flowers, they headed over the lawns towards the salon. It was a beautiful warm day with a gentle breeze, and Atlas took great lungfuls of the sweet air. He knew how lucky he was to be living here but he couldn't help feeling unsettled. With Thor so gloomy, and Māui hiding himself away, there was a lot on his mind. He just wished things would go back to how they had been before Loki's arrival. Maybe if he just got everyone together to talk things through and call a truce in this silly war of tricks . . .

The salon was busier than Atlas had ever seen it, with gods and goddesses making wreaths. Venus sat in the styling chair, calling out orders. Her long, lustrous tresses flowed down behind her.

"Atlas," Ari said sharply. "Don't just stand there. Get to work."

"You're not the boss of me," Atlas replied angrily. "*MAKE A WREATH*!" Venus snapped. She could be as scary as she was beautiful.

Atlas grabbed a handful of flowers, clumsily trying to form them into a ring. He saw Ari smirk at him triumphantly and he stuck his tongue out at her.

As Atlas worked on his wreath, he saw Māui nip in through the door, carrying a pair of scissors. Atlas guessed he wanted to help pick flowers.

"Māui!" he said, cheerily, waving at his friend.

But then he blinked in surprise as Māui scurried up behind Venus's chair and, quick as a flash, CHOPPED her flowing hair off. He roared with laughter. Then he winked at Atlas and sauntered out of the salon.

There was a moment of horrified silence as everyone stared at Venus in disbelief. And then . . .

"AARRRGHHHH!"

Venus clutched her shorn head and screamed.

Mars came thundering across the lawn, drawn by the screams of his beloved Venus. Atlas tried to explain what had just happened but Mars was in no mood to listen.

"My love," Mars cried, falling to his knees. "My darling Venus, what has become of your hair? Who has done this to you?"

Venus fell into his arms. "It was the

trickster Māui," she cried.

"It wasn't!" protested Atlas. He had recognised that wink. He was sure it was Loki, up to his tricks. Māui wouldn't do something that mean.

"Everyone saw it," said Venus.

"I shall destroy him!" Mars vowed. "He will be punished for this. I will rouse my father Zeus if necessary. Māui will toil day and night to make you a crown of red tresses, to replace your beautiful hair."

"Hold on," Atlas said. "Māui would never—"

"I've got it!" interrupted a voice. All eyes turned to the doorway, to be greeted by the sight of Māui, carrying half a pineapple with a straw in it. He grinned at Atlas triumphantly. "Itching powder in Loki's underpants. He'll never . . ."

Māui trailed off, noticing everyone glaring at him. "What's going on?" he asked.

In reply, Mars roared and launched himself across the room, slamming into Māui. Someone screamed. The two of them thudded into the wall then spun and staggered across the room, scattering flowers everywhere.

"It wasn't Māui," Atlas cried. "It was Loki!" But no one was listening to him.

Mars stood on a chair and performed a

leap, right on top of the sprawled Māui, like a WWE wrestler. Māui went *OOF* as the wind was knocked out of him. Atlas winced.

"Get him, Mars!" someone shouted. Atlas wasn't at all surprised to see it was Loki, who had reappeared. He caught Atlas's eye and winked again, confirming all of Atlas's suspicions.

The fight didn't last long. Māui was strong, but taken off guard, and Mars was the god of war after all. Ari was the one to put a stop to it. She dived in front of Māui, protecting him.

"Enough," she said, holding up her hand. Atlas gave his sister a grateful nod.

Mars stopped, though he didn't look happy

about it. He went to check on Venus, who was sobbing. As Ari swept up the crushed flower petals strewn all over the floor, Atlas helped his battered friend out of the salon.

"**Two-nil**!" called a smug voice behind them as they limped back to Māui's room.

Atlas shuddered. At this rate Loki was going to score a hat-trick and there didn't seem to be anything Atlas, or anyone else, could do to stop him.

CHAPTER ★ ★
TEN

"Hey, Māui, are you in there?" Atlas called, knocking on Māui's door. His friend hadn't been at breakfast and he was worried about him.

Atlas banged on the door. There was no answer, but he heard some crashes and clunks from inside so he went in anyway.

Māui had a suitcase in the middle of

the room and was hurling things into it. His Hawai'ian shirts, his board shorts, a pineapple, his surfboard, his skateboard, his flip flops, another pineapple, his fish-hook, a hat shaped like a pineapple.

"What's going on?" Atlas asked.

"What does it look like?" Māui said bitterly. "I'm packing to go back to Hawai'i, where I don't have to worry about getting beaten up or thrown out of windows every day."

"You can't leave," Atlas said. "Who will I hang out with?"

"Sorry, little dude," Māui said. "But there just isn't room in this hotel for two tricksters. Loki won, fair and square."

"Not exactly fair and square," Atlas said.

"Well, that's tricksters for you," Māui said. "I guess we're just bad people."

"You're not like Loki," Atlas said. "His tricks are mean-spirited. They hurt people. You just try to make people laugh. You make everything fun. It's not the same."

But Māui didn't answer. He had his back turned to Atlas.

"Did you hear what I said?" Atlas said. "I don't want you to go. You're my best friend. Ever. I don't want to lose you."

Māui still hadn't turned around. Atlas grabbed his friend's shoulder, turning the demigod around. Then he stood, shocked at what he saw.

Māui was crying.

"I've . . ." Māui sniffled. "I've never had a best friend before."

"Well," Atlas said, suddenly awkward. "Neither have I, to be honest."

"I had my brothers," Māui said. "And my cousins. And my second cousins. And my mum and dad. And their brothers. And sisters. And THEIR cousins, and . . .."

"I get it," Atlas said.

"But that's family," Māui said. "They had no choice but to like me."

Atlas shuffled his feet, embarrassed, but with a warm feeling in his stomach at the same time.

"You're the only person who ever chose to be friends with me," Māui continued, sniffing loudly.

"So you'll stay?" Atlas asked hopefully.

"I'd like to. But what about Loki?!" Māui asked.

"I'll take care of Loki," Atlas said.

"What are you going to do? Beat him up?"

"No."

"Trick him into jumping off a cliff?"

"No."

"Bury him under a mountain?"

"No."

"So what are you going to do?"

"I'm going to reason with him," Atlas said.

Māui frowned. "Good luck with that, little dude."

Atlas marched outside and found Loki lying on a sun lounger drinking a glass of Ambrosia and looking very pleased with himself.

"Ah, Atlas!" Loki said. "How wonderful to see you. Has Māui withdrawn from the prank contest yet?"

"Yes," Atlas said. "The contest is silly. It's dumb for us all to be fighting and trying to get each other in trouble. I believe that, deep down, you are a good person. Am I right?"

Loki had stopped smiling. He looked at Atlas, thoughtful.

"No one has ever thought I might be a good person," he said. "Not when they've gotten to know me."

"Maybe that's all you need," Atlas said, feeling encouraged. "Someone who believes in you. Maybe you ARE good, deep down."

Loki stared into his drink and was silent for a long time. Then he looked up at Atlas with a wicked grin on his face. "Nah," he said.

Atlas stepped back, shocked.

"I am who I am, Atlas," Loki said. "I've looked deep down and there's nothing good in me. Just tricks. And I am going to carry on playing tricks on Māui until he is utterly destroyed. Because that is what I do."

Then the trickster god lay back and took another sip of his drink, sighing happily.

Atlas walked away, his stomach churning with anger. "OK, you asked for it, Loki," he muttered to himself. "I gave you a chance, but you threw it in my face. I'm going to make your life a misery until you leave this hotel."

So it began, **OPERATION GOODBYE LOKI.**

The first part of the plan consisted of Atlas offering to help out with serving breakfast. Mum and Dad agreed straight away.

Loki liked to have eggs every morning. But Atlas had a surprise for him. He'd been downstairs to visit Hades that morning to get some very special eggs. **Hippogriff eggs.** Atlas had had a fiery encounter with a hippogriff once, and they were extremely powerful creatures, their insides like a furnace.

"I hope you like your eggs hot," he said, placing a platter in front of Loki. He whipped off the cover to reveal a plateful of huge eggs, burning fiercely. The room went quiet as everyone watched to see what Loki would do.

But Loki didn't shriek or run away as Atlas had hoped. He didn't get angry or thrust the plate away in disgust as Atlas had expected. Instead he clapped his hands together in excitement.

"I do!" Loki cried. "I DO like them hot."

And before Atlas's astonished eyes, he gobbled the burning eggs down without complaint. "Delicious!" Loki exclaimed. "**HOT AND SPICY**! Is there something to wash it down with?"

Atlas frowned. This wasn't quite how he'd imagined things panning out. But Atlas wasn't defeated yet.

"I'll bring you some mead," he said.

Atlas stalked back into the kitchen and, with a mischievous grin, he scooped up a tankard full of herring brine and took it back out to Loki. The brine stank of fish, sharp enough to make Atlas's eyes water. He set it down on the table. Loki picked up the tankard, winked at Atlas and slurped down the brine.

Then he stared up at Atlas with a look of surprise on his face.

Atlas grinned. "Did you like your mead, Loki?"

"What vintage is this?" Loki asked.

"W-what?" Atlas replied, confounded.

"It is the finest mead I've tasted from your cellars," Loki said with a sly grin.

Atlas's shoulders dropped. He stared at Loki in disbelief. It was impossible to get the better of him. He grunted in annoyance and stomped back into the kitchens. His plan wasn't working. But he still wasn't done. He had one more thing up his sleeve.

Atlas brought out a massive silver serving platter with a domed cover.

"A special dish for our guest of honour," he cried.

He placed it in front of Loki, then he whipped off the cover to reveal . . .

"**COCKROACHES**!" Loki screeched.

The dish was awash with hundreds of scurrying insects: some fat, some tiny, some huge, some hairy.

Loki shrieked and clapped a hand over his mouth.

Atlas grinned. Finally, he had hit the target. It looked like he'd found Loki's weakness.

"MY FAVOURITE!" Loki squealed. "How did you know?!" He grabbed a handful of roaches and shoved them into his mouth, chewing furiously, their cases and legs

crunching between his teeth. "Ooh, there are African bluebacks. And Russian shortlegs! Exquisite!"

Atlas stared in astonishment as Loki munched the insects. *How has this happened?* he thought. *How has defeat been snatched from the jaws of victory?* Loki held out a particularly revolting-looking cockroach with waggling legs towards Atlas. Still chewing he said, "You've GOT to try one of these."

"No thanks," Atlas said, backing away.

"You're missing out!" Loki called after him. **"I LOVE IT HERE AT THE HOTEL OF THE GODS! I WILL NEVER LEAVE. DO YOU HEAR ME? NEVER!"**

★ ★ CHAPTER ★ ★
ELEVEN

A tlas sat in the kitchen on Midsummer's
Day, staring at one of Hades'
inspirational quotes on a slate over the stove.
It read:

> *A pinch of patience.*
> *A dash of kindness.*
> *A spoonful of laughter.*
> *A sprinkle of death.*

Atlas felt defeated. He felt deflated. He'd been sitting there for ages, racking his brains for something else. Another plan. Another trick. But he wasn't Māui, he just wasn't good at this sort of thing.

The smell of brine was making Atlas feel ill, but there were more important things to consider. There had to be a way to get the better of Loki. There had to be a way to make him look a fool. If he couldn't think of it, Māui was certain to leave instead of Loki.

Ari came in. At first she sniffed and walked on. But then she stopped, came back and looked at him.

"Are you OK?" she asked.

"Not really," Atlas replied. "Māui wants to leave because of Loki. I need to find a way to convince Loki to leave instead and I just can't think of anything."

Ari frowned. "Well," she said. "Māui's not my favourite person, and to be honest, Atlas, you haven't been winning any Best Brother Awards lately. I still haven't forgotten the swimming pool incident."

"I'm sorry about that. Māui and I can be pretty annoying, I know," Atlas said, simply. "But he's my friend. How would you feel if it was Venus wanting to leave?"

Ari sighed. "I don't know what the answer to your problem is," she said. "But the best place to go when you're looking for answers is always the library."

Atlas brightened. "That's it!" he cried. "The library!" And he raced for the door.

To his great surprise, he found Thor there, sitting with Quetzalcóatl. They were surrounded by piles of dusty books.

"You're reading?" Atlas asked Thor in surprise.

"No," Thor replied. "I'm just hiding from Loki. He'll never think to look for me in a library."

"Why are you here, Quetzalcóatl?" Atlas asked cautiously. The last time he'd seen the Aztec god in the library, he'd been researching how to cook human flesh!

"I am the Aztec god of wisdom," Quetzalcóatl replied, somewhat huffily.

"Sorry," Atlas said. "I didn't mean to be rude. What are you reading there?"

Quetzalcóatl looked a bit sheepish. "It's called *Cooking the French*."

"You mean, *Cooking, the French Way*?" Atlas asked.

"No. *Cooking the French*. There's an art to cooking French people, you see. They can be rather tough and a little salty."

"I see," Atlas said shortly. Then he shook his head and decided to move on. "I need to research a way to get rid of Loki," he said.

"He must have a weakness."

"Sounds great," Thor said. "Let me know if you need some help with . . ." He looked at the piles of books thoughtfully. ". . . with carrying anything."

"I shall assist," Quetzalcóatl said, to Atlas's surprise. He walked over to a shelf and took down a huge stack of books, dropping them on the table with a thud. "These are the books about Norse mythology."

"Thanks, buddy," Atlas said, grinning. "Can I call you that?"

"No," Quetzalcóatl replied.

"OK, fair enough," Atlas said. He sat at the desk and pulled one of the books over to him.

Quetzalcóatl did the same. Thor also took a book and opened it, peering intently at the page.

"You're holding that upside down," Quetzalcóatl said.

"I know," Thor said quickly. "I like to challenge myself."

"The problem with Loki is he's not

frightened of anything," Atlas said, flicking through one of the dusty old books.

"Except for Odin, that is," Thor said. He picked up a huge pile of books and began lifting them like they were a set of weights. "Odin once chained him to a rock and had a serpent drip poison into his eyes, just for spilling orange juice on the hall carpet."

"Loki's screams could be heard halfway around the world," Quetzalcóatl added. "I even heard them in Mexico. I believe he would do anything to avoid repeating such torment. But only Odin would have the power to chain him to a rock. And Odin isn't here."

Then Atlas froze. A thought had just occurred to him. He looked up at Thor and Quetzalcóatl and pursed his lips.

"I think I might have a plan," he said after a moment. "But it won't be easy to pull off."

"The basement?!" Venus said, looking around the gloomy room, disdain dripping from her voice. "This place is literally the pits. No offence," she said to Hades, who lived there.

"None taken," Hades said cheerfully.

Atlas had invited the gods and goddesses to a secret meeting. No one seemed particularly delighted to be there, all crammed in together in the basement. Thor and Mars glared angrily at Māui. Atlas had told them the truth about the tricks Loki had pulled while pretending to be Māui, but they were still suspicious.

Hades was the only one smiling. He was pleased to have some company in his basement at last. He was fussing around and bringing out tea, assisted by Alexa, his chief demon. "It's so lovely to have some guests," he said. "So glad you could come. Have a French Fancy, they're lighter than air. Alexa, some milk for Bastet please, and more tea!"

"Do you have any fingers?" Quetzalcóatl asked.

"Erm, do you mean chocolate fingers?"

Hades said nervously.

"Ah, forget it," Quetzalcóatl said with a sigh.

Venus shivered and pulled a face, looking around at the metal-streaked walls. Heavy metal music throbbed somewhere in the background and the faint whiff of sulphur could be detected coming from a passage which Atlas knew led to the very gates of hell itself. He noticed a tapestry hung on the wall, which read:

You don't have to be dead to work here, but it helps!

Apart from Hades, only Cerbie seemed happy down in the basement – his old home, back when he had three heads. He rushed around for a while then lay down next to a grating, from which warm air emanated, along with the occasional scream of some poor, damned soul.

"Sorry there aren't enough seats," Hades said to Venus. "But you can sit on this stack of skulls if you like?"

"I'm fine, thanks," Venus replied with a thin smile, then she turned to Atlas. "Why ARE we in the basement?"

"Because everyone hates coming down here," Atlas explained. Then he looked at

Hades and added, "No offence."

"None taken," Hades replied, offering him a snack bowl. "Pomegranate seed?"

"No thanks," Atlas said. "Look, we all know why we're here. We need to get rid of Loki, once and for all. Agreed?"

The gods and goddesses exchanged uncertain looks.

"Venus, he cut off your hair," said Atlas.

Venus touched her cropped hair and nodded unhappily.

"Thor, he stole your hammer," Atlas said.

Thor nodded sullenly.

"Māui, he tricked people into thinking you did these terrible things," continued Atlas.

Māui looked at his arms and legs. "I'm still covered in bruises because of him."

"He chased me," Bastet said, twitching her tail.

"He burned the maypole too," Ari added.

"He swapped my sugar for salt," Dad said.

Everyone murmured in agreement.

"He told me my jokes weren't funny," Hades said.

Everyone looked at each other and shrugged.

"**Loki is a real pain**," Atlas said. "I think I

know a way to get rid of him. But I'm going to need all of you to help. And there's not much time to pull it together."

"Go on," Bastet said. "We're with you, Atlas."

"OK," Atlas said. He took a deep breath. "Dad, I need you to get rid of Loki for a few hours. Tell him we need more fish."

"Atlas my boy, we do NOT need more fish," Dad said. He looked haunted. "I can't pickle any more. I have a headache, a backache and a noseache from all this brine."

"We need to get him away from the hotel for a few hours," Atlas said. "Loki loves fishing and he'll be desperate to remind everyone how good he is at it."

Dad sighed. "OK. But this means you eat fish for breakfast, lunch and dinner for the next three weeks."

"Agreed," Atlas said.

Atlas turned to Thor next.

"Thor, I need you to go to the mountains and bring me back a huge boulder."

Thor gave him a thumbs up.

Atlas pointed to his sister and Venus in turn. "The two of you, to the salon please." Then he turned to Māui. "Find your fish-hook, we're going to need it."

"I suppose you want me to fight Loki," said Mars, flexing his muscles.

"No," replied Atlas. "You're going to the salon too."

Mars started to protest, but Atlas had moved on to Quetzalcóatl.

"We're going to need some of those snakes again— **NOT YET**!" Atlas cried as an asp started writhing around on the floor.

Sighing, Quetzalcóatl made it disappear.

"What about me?"

Hades asked, looking downcast at being excluded.

Atlas turned to him. "You have the most important job of all," he said, clapping one hand on Hades' shoulder. "You're putting the band back together. **IT'S SHOWTIME!**"

The next couple of hours were a frenzy of activity. But for once, the gods and goddesses worked together, as a team.

Finally, they were ready to execute the plan. Atlas stood outside with the late-afternoon sun warming his back. He saw Loki come trotting back across the fields, whistling happily, another huge sack over his shoulders stuffed with herring.

When he was sure Loki was in earshot, Atlas gave the signal.

The music started up. Hades led a sixty-strong band of demons, dressed in the furs of Asgard and holding horns, trumpets and drums. They played a fanfare, followed by "For He's a Jolly Good Fellow".

Atlas saw Loki stop dead, squinting ahead into the setting sun, trying to work out what was going on.

Please let my plan work, Atlas thought.

Mars stepped on to the stage that had been set up for the Midsummer concert. But he didn't look like he usually did. Venus and

Ari had done their work, and done it well. Mars now sported long, flowing grey hair. He wore a great winged helmet, forged for him by Hades. Beside him stood a large grey wolf, Freki, with slavering jaws and a wicked gleam in his eyes. (Freki was actually Cerbie in disguise.)

"ALL HAIL ODIN!" cried Bastet. "King of the Gods of Asgard."

Loki stared up at Mars uncertainly. "Odin?" he asked. "Did you come for the party?"

Now it was time for the final touch. With a faint nod of his head, "Odin" signalled to Māui, who was hiding behind a hedge on the other side of the garden. Māui held one end of a fishing line. The other end of it was way up high in the clouds. Māui hauled at the line with all his might, dragging a fat, black cloud across the sky.

The sun darkened. Thor threw his hammer and lightning flashed from the cloud. There was a loud rumble of thunder.

Atlas was hidden behind the stage, holding a microphone. He turned it on and spoke, pretending to be Odin. "Loki!" he roared, his voice booming from the big speakers. Hades, standing behind a mixing desk with earphones on, twiddled some dials to add bass and reverb to make it sound extra deep and powerful. "I have had reports that you

have been impersonating me," "Odin" roared.

Loki looked terrified and fell to his knees. Another bolt of lightning flashed from the cloud, followed by an ominous rumble of thunder.

"I have also heard you have been playing tricks on the residents of this hotel," "Odin" went on.

"But . . . but . . . I . . ." Loki spluttered. Then he stopped and looked up at Mars, a hint of suspicion in his eye.

"How . . ." he began. ". . . How can I be certain it is you, Father?" he asked.

Oh, he's clever, Atlas thought.

"WHAT?!" "Odin" roared back at Loki.

Atlas knew he had to hold his nerve. This was all part of the plan. He just hoped that Mars wouldn't lose his temper and give the game away.

"It . . . it's just . . ." Loki went on, rising to his feet. "I'm not the one who's been playing tricks, you see. The evil demigod Māui has been causing trouble around here. I need to make sure it is really you, and that you are not Māui in disguise."

"And how do you propose we do that?" "Odin" asked. Atlas made sure his voice dripped with more venom than one of Quetzalcóatl's snakes.

"Perhaps you could come down from your

horse and we could sit together, drink mead, eat pickled herring and talk this through," Loki wheedled, stepping closer.

There was a deathly silence. The assembled gods shuffled slightly and gave each other looks. It seemed reasonable.

Then Atlas spoke again. Softer this time.

"Why would you say this to me, your king?" he began. "Why would you propose we eat pickled herring together . . ."

"Well . . ." Loki tried to interrupt. But "Odin" hadn't finished.

"**. . . WHEN YOU KNOW THAT I, ODIN, KING OF THE GODS OF ASGARD, AM ALLERGIC TO PICKLED HERRING!**" Atlas roared.

Hades turned up the volume and the reverb nearly blasted Loki off his feet.

Loki fell to his knees. "I'm sorry, oh king," he pleaded. "I forgot."

"Bring me chains!" "Odin" commanded.

"Ch-chains?" Loki spluttered.

Venus and Bastet stepped forward, struggling between them to carry a huge coil of clanking metal chain with a great ring on the end.

"Thor! Bring me the rock."

"R . . . rock?" Loki whined.

Thor picked up a massive boulder lying behind the stage. He carried it back and dropped it down in front of Loki. The ground shook and Loki wailed.

"**Tie this fool to the rock**," "Odin" went on.

Grinning from ear to ear, Thor reached out for Loki, grabbing him by the shoulder and dragging him towards the boulder.

"And now," "Odin" went on. "**Summon me a serpent**. The more poisonous the better."

"Finally!" Quetzalcóatl cried. And with that, he transformed into the fattest, longest, creepiest, toothiest snake anyone had ever seen. He stretched up, towering over Loki,

179

venom dripping from his wickedly sharp fangs.

"**NOOOOOOO**," Loki cried in horror at the sight. He leapt up, breaking free of Thor's grip, and sprinted as fast as his legs would carry him back down the path towards the cove where the Viking ship was moored.

"**Come on**," Māui cried with delight. "**Let's get him!**" The other gods and goddesses chased after Loki.

Atlas grinned as he watched Loki tripping down the narrow steps to the beach and leaping into the longship. A moment later, the sails unfurled.

"Let's give him a little helping hand, shall

we?" Thor asked Māui.

Māui nodded and hauled on the fishing line, dragging the cloud along. Thor flung his hammer directly into the middle of it and another lightning bolt crackled down with a bang and a flash, hitting the longship's mast.

"**Owwww**!" Loki howled in pain as he scurried around the deck, pulling ropes and hauling sails. Then a huge wind swept up and sent the longship scudding over the waves and out to sea.

Atlas watched with satisfaction as the ship grew smaller and smaller and eventually disappeared over the horizon. He turned to his friends and grinned. **OPERATION**

GOODBYE LOKI had been a success.

"Game," Māui said.

"Set," Thor went on.

"Match," finished Atlas.

CHAPTER TWELVE

"Do you know what we eat at celebrations in Mexico?" Quetzalcóatl asked.

"Let me guess," Atlas said. "Roasted human legs? Fried human hands? Boiled human brains?"

"Don't be disgusting," Quetzalcóatl replied, grimacing in distaste. "Everyone knows boiled human brains taste foul."

"Sorry," Atlas said.

"We eat tamales," Quetzalcóatl explained. "And corn on the cob."

"Of course," Atlas said.

The **MIDSUMMER'S NIGHT CELEBRATION** was in full swing, with music, food, decorations and a vigorous tournament of Kubb, a game which involved hurling wooden batons at wooden blocks to try and knock them over. The hotel's residents had dressed up, with flower wreaths in their hair. Venus looked particularly radiant with her new short hairstyle, skilfully styled by Ari in the salon.

"You did a good job, Ari," Atlas said, going over to his sister.

"So did you, Atlas," she said, putting a flower wreath on his head. "I'm sorry I was mean to you."

"Well, I'm sorry about the tricks Māui and I played on you."

"Tricks are funny for a while," Ari said. "But sometimes they can go too far, and then it takes a lot of effort to put things right."

"You can say that again," said Atlas.

"COME AND EAT!" Dad shouted.

The long table had been rebuilt and was now groaning under the weight of all the food: new potatoes with sour cream and dill, fresh strawberries, mead and fruit juice to drink. And of course, piles and piles of surprisingly delicious pickled herring! Atlas's dad had not wanted to waste the extra fish Loki had brought back so he'd ended up pickling that too. Now every spare bedroom in the hotel was full to bursting with sealed jars of pickled herring. They'd had to store some in the stables, in the salon and even down in Hades' basement.

Atlas's dad, however, was not eating.

"I never want to look at another herring," he said, sipping a cup of mead.

After everyone had eaten their fill, the demon band struck up and played a fast jig called "Goodbye Loki" that got everyone up and dancing. Thor danced with Venus until a jealous Mars cut in. Mum danced with Dad, who had perhaps overdone it on the mead and was now leaping around like a fool. Ari danced with Māui. Bastet slunk about on her own (as all cat owners know, cats like to be AROUND people but not actually WITH people). Even Quetzalcóatl hopped around to the beat, his great feathered headdress floating in the warm summer air behind him.

Māui came over to Atlas and handed him a pickling jar.

"Not more herring," Atlas said with a groan. "I mean I like it, but I've had plenty already—"

"It's not herring," Māui said with a grin. Then his face grew serious. "It's a Midsummer gift, from me to you."

"Oh, you didn't need to get me anything," Atlas said, feeling touched. It wasn't like Māui to make kind gestures like this.

"Of course I did," Māui said. "If it weren't for you, Atlas, I would have left the hotel for good, and Loki would still be here making everyone's life a misery. I just wanted to say thank you. You've been a really good friend. My best friend, actually."

Atlas felt himself choking up a bit. He gave Māui a hug. "You're my best friend too."

Māui clapped him on the back. "Go on," he said. "Open your gift."

Atlas popped the metal clip. The lid sprang open and a huge, hairy spider jumped out, clamping itself on to Atlas's face.

Atlas shrieked and fell backwards, landing on the trestle table, which collapsed under him. A huge pile of pickled herring slid down and buried him in a wet, slimy, briny mess.

"Gotcha!" said Māui, giggling.

Atlas sat up, brushing the spider off

his face, and then . . . he began to laugh too. Sitting on a bed of fish under the

Midsummer's Night sky, he laughed and laughed and laughed.

When Atlas had laughed so much his sides ached, Māui reached out his hand and helped Atlas up. There was a huge grin on his face, and the bonfire's reflection twinkled in his eyes.

"There's only room for one trickster at the

Hotel of the Gods," Māui told Atlas. "And that's me."

Atlas wouldn't have had it any other way.

Ha! **Ha!** **Ha!** **Ha!**

COMING SOON

HOTEL
OF THE
GODS

Aztec
Chocolate
Meltdown

TOM
EASTON

A CHOC-TASTIC NEW HOTEL OF THE GODS ADVENTURE!